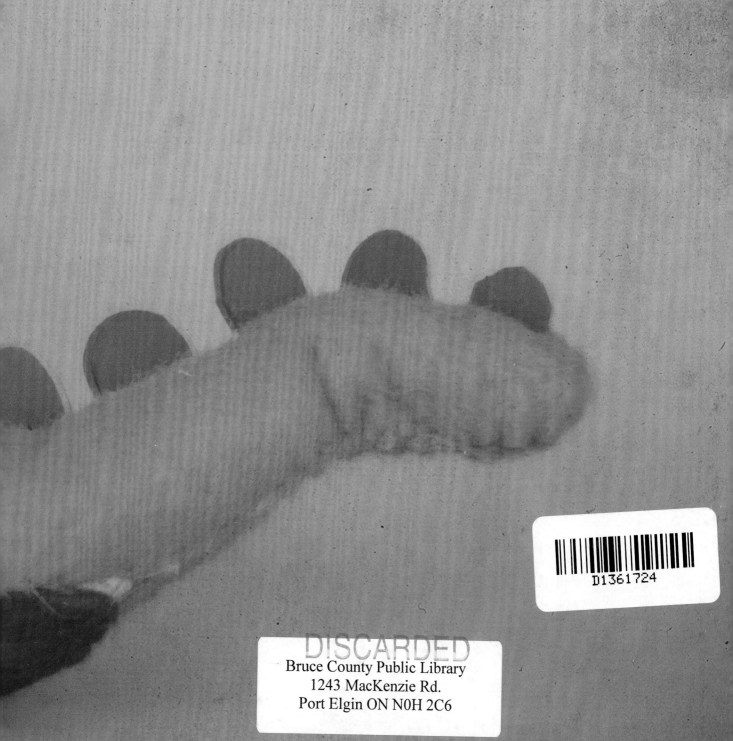

First published in Belgium and Holland by Clavis Uitgeverij, Hasselt – Amsterdam, 2013
Copyright © 2013, Clavis Uitgeverij

English translation from the Dutch by Clavis Publishing Inc. New York
Copyright © 2014 for the English language edition: Clavis Publishing Inc. New York

Visit us on the web at www.clavisbooks.com

The Cuddle Dragon written and illustrated by Axel Janssens
Original title: Kobe en de knuffeldraak
Translated from the Dutch by Clavis Publishing

ISBN 978-1-60537-184-9

This book was printed in March 2014 at Proost, Everdongenlaan 23, 2300 Turnhout, Belgium

First Edition
10 9 8 7 6 5 4 3 2 1

Axel Janssens

THE CUDDLE DRAGON

Clavis
NEW YORK

"Ding dong!"
The doorbell sounds.

Leo hurries down the flight of stairs.
"I'll get it, I'll get it!" he yells.
He is very happy. Tomorrow he'll be
six years old. That's very big. Today all his
friends are coming for a sleepover. And tomorrow?
Tomorrow there's a **big party!**

Ben and **Carl** are the first to ring the bell,
but soon **Lucy** and **Sophie** arrive too.
Then comes **Gregory. Kenny** is the last to arrive.

He has brought a **big gift**,
with a ribbon around it.
Leo is very curious to see what it might be.

The party doesn't start till tomorrow, but the house is already full of fun.
There are pancakes for dinner and decorations everywhere.

Before going to bed they all build
a castle with sheets and pillows.
It's so big everyone can fit!

Kenny takes something from his backpack.
It's a big green cuddle toy.
"Haha, look at that!" Leo laughs.
"Kenny has a cuddle toy!"

"That's not a cuddle toy," Kenny answers.
"That's my best friend Pepper.
He goes everywhere I go and it's always fun.
And whenever there's danger, Pepper protects me.
So I never have to be afraid."

"Ha!" Leo says. "Never **afraid**, huh?
Not even of the Bed Beast?"
"The Bed Beast..." Carl repeats.

"The...**Bed Beast,**"
Leo whispers with a grin on his face.

"The Bed Beast lives under your bed
and tickles your toes when you are almost asleep.
He has about twenty eyes and he eats
your slippers... Sometimes you can
even hear him **smack** his lips...."

Carl's eyes open up wide and Gregory gulps.
"Haha," Kenny **laughs**. "Nothing scary about a Bed Beast."

"Pepper is very big and heavy.
When he jumps on the bed,
the Bed Beast will make another noise.
Before you know it he'll be flattened,
just you wait."

The kids laugh really hard.
All except Leo....

"Oh yeah?" Leo says.

"Have you ever heard of the Closet Monster?"

Everyone is silent. **"The Closet Monster is a very dangerous animal,"**

Leo tells.

"He looks like a normal closet,
but he has over a **thousand sharp teeth**
and a **big, dirty tongue,** which he uses to try to lick you.
And sometimes, if you listen carefully, you can hear him
breathing at night.

Crrrrack...

Crrraaaack...

Crrrrrraaack...
the Closet says."

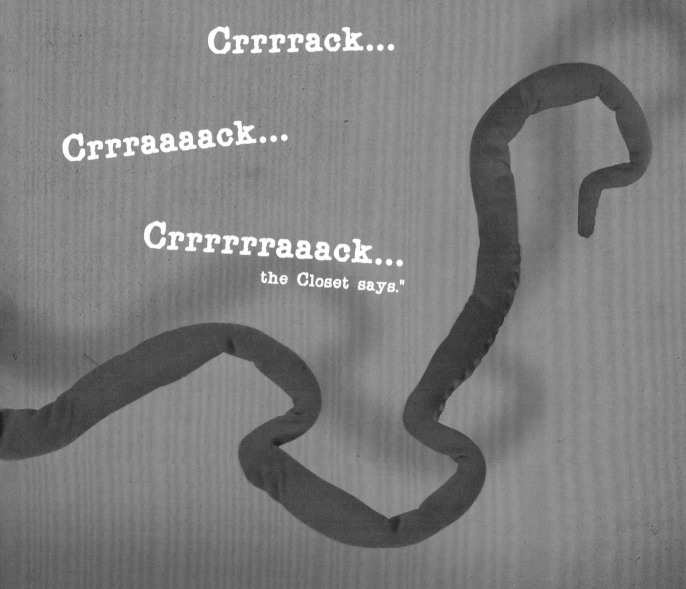

Sophie cuddles up against her big sister.

Ben and Gregory exchange frightened looks and Carl bites his lip.

But Kenny is not afraid.

"That will be funny!" he laughs.

"The Closet Monster is made out of wood.

He doesn't know that Pepper can spit fire.

Pepper will burn the Closet Monster's bum...."

"Hahaha," everyone laughs.

They can imagine what that would look like.

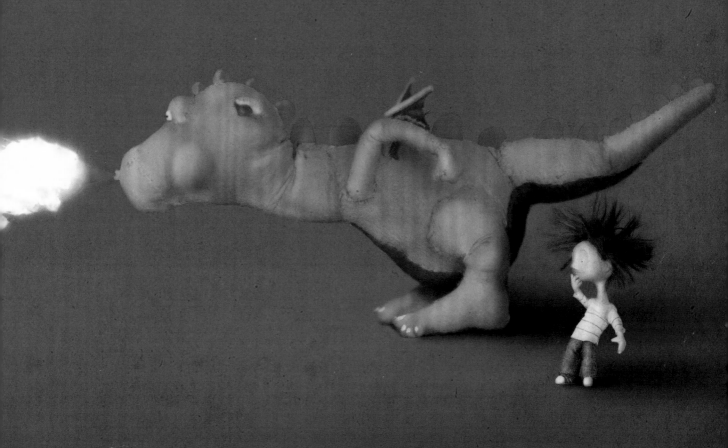

But Leo is getting a bit **upset**.
"Yes well," he says **loudly**,
"I still have to tell you about the
scariest monster.

Outside, in the trees, lives
the **Ogre of the Woods,**
a beast that's about ten feet long,
with thick matted fur. He has
big yellow eyes with which
he can see in the dark and he
has **long claws** to grab you.

He rattles the windows and
scratches the doors. His favorite
meal is little children, and he's
always hungry."

Now it's very quiet. Ben bites his pillow.
Carl takes a gulp of juice and
Sophie hides underneath the sheets.

"Hey, you don't have to be afraid, you know,"

Kenny soothes them.

"Pepper can fly, and when the Ogre of the Woods comes, we can climb
on Pepper's back and fly up high. From there we can throw
tomatoes and mud at the ogre. He won't know what's hit him."

Everyone thinks that's very funny.
Carl laughs so much, juice
comes out his nose. And
then everyone laughs
even harder.

It's getting late
and everyone goes to bed, still laughing.
But Leo is sulking. **Ugh**, he thinks,
my scary stories aren't funny,
and then he falls asleep too....

But suddenly Leo is wide awake.

Something is tickling his toes....

Huh? A Bed Beast?

He lies completely still, his eyes open wide.

Again, something tickles his toes. Then the cat jumps onto his bed!

Leo is startled, but he thinks: **Phew! It's not the Bed Beast.**

But then he hears something.... **"Crrrr.... Crrrrr.... Crrrrr...."**

It sounds just like the Closet Monster he was talking about. **"Crrrr.... Crrrr...."**

"Oh no," Leo shakes. **The Closet Monster is here.**

He squeezes his eyes shut. **"Crrr.... Crrrr...."**

Carefully, Leo looks over the edge of the bed. The closet isn't moving.

Crrr.... Crrr.... Crrr.... It's Carl who is snoring. **Phew!** Leo thinks.

TAP…TAP…TAP. Leo jumps. **TAP…TAP…TAP,**
he hears against the window. Leo peeks out from under his blanket.
He sees a big hand with long fingers tapping on the window.
"Whoa! The Ogre of the Woods!" Leo shrieks
and everyone wakes with a start. Kenny switches on the lights.

The wind is blowing a branch from the big tree
against the window. It goes TAP...TAP...TAP....
Leo wipes the tears from his eyes.
He is still shaking.

When everyone is asleep, Kenny whispers to Leo:

"You might want to open my gift now. It will come in handy."

He gives Leo the **big present.**

Leo carefully unwraps it and lifts the lid from the box.

His eyes light up and he smiles through his tears.

In the box is a big cuddle toy. Wait. It's not a cuddle toy,

it's a **big, tough dragon.**

"He has sharp teeth that can bite through anything," Kenny says,

"and strong claws so he can run really quickly and jump really high.

And of course he can **spit fire....**"

"So beautiful," Leo says.

"I will call him Fred,

Fred the Terrible."

The house is quiet, everyone is asleep.
Every now and then you hear: "Smack smack....
Crrr.... Crrr...." or "TAP...TAP...TAP...." But it doesn't bother Leo.
He is holding his new friend tight.

Tomorrow there'll be a **big party,**
but already this is the **best birthday he's ever had**....